בס"ד

This Book Belongs To:

לה' הארץ ומלואה

Matthew Hamburger

Please read it to me!

YOSSI & LAIBEL ON THE BALL

by Dina Rosenfeld

illustrated by Norman Nodel

Hachai
PUBLISHING

Dedicated to our beloved children
Rivkah Malka, Daniella Esther,
Meir and Rayzel

☙❧

Pamela and George Rohr

☙❧

Yossi and Laibel
On the Ball

To all my sisters-in-law...with love. D.R.

✳

In memory of my parents, Rabbi Mordechai and Mrs. Sarah Nodel. N.N.

FIRST EDITION
May 1998 / Iyar 5758

Library of Congress Catalog Card Number: 97-75102
ISBN # 0-922613-83-4

Hachai Publishing
156 Chester Avenue • Brooklyn, New York 11218
Tel 718-633-0100 • Fax 718-633-0103 • www.hachai.com

Printed in Hong Kong

Special thanks to Eileen Turko, Director of the N.Y. State Parks Games for the Physically Challenged, for all the helpful information.

Yossi and Laibel went outside to play
In their backyard on a lovely spring day.
Yossi pitched; Laibel swung at the ball - what a whack!
His bat hit the ball with an earsplitting crack!

The baseball popped up; it flew so far away
That it seemed like it wouldn't come down the same day.
"Wow!" Yossi cried. "It sailed over the wall!
How are we going to get back our ball?"

"Here it is!" said a voice that the boys didn't know.
"I'll help you out and give it a throw!"
"Thanks," Laibel called. "Who are you, anyway?"
Said the voice, "My name's Avi; I moved in today,
And baseball's my favorite, so what do you say,
If I get my mitt, do you mind if I play?"

"But how," Laibel asked, "can you play in a chair?"
"Well, it moves," Avi said. "It takes me everywhere.
My legs aren't so strong, but my pitching arm's great!
I'll be happy to show you – just stay there and wait."

"I don't know," whispered Laibel to Yossi. "Do you?
What exactly do you think this new kid can do?"
Yossi said, "It's a mitzvah to love every Jew
Although he may look a bit different from you.
How he looks on the outside won't count in the end,
It's what he's like inside that makes him a friend."

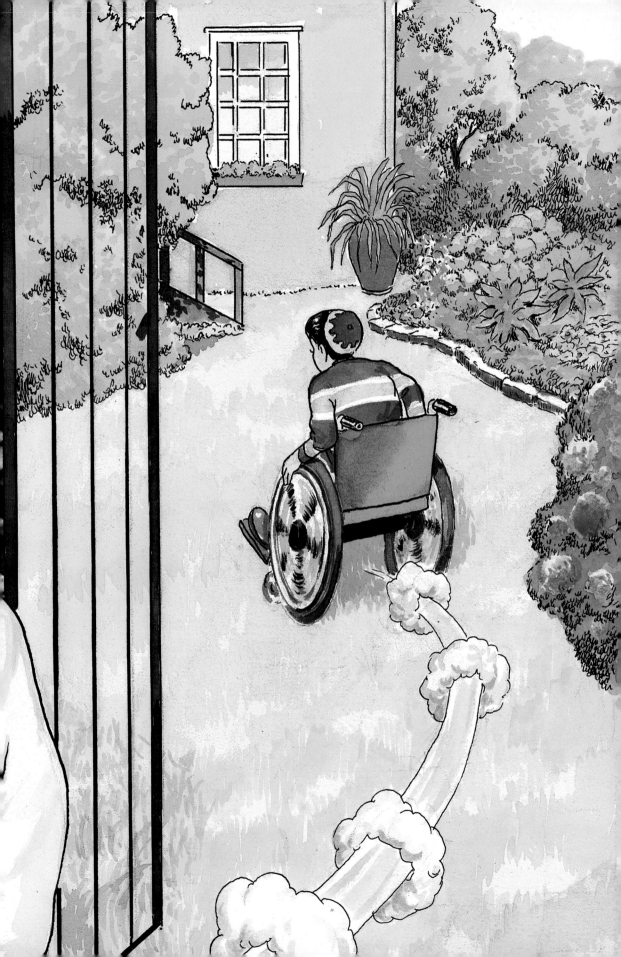

"I'm back!" Avi called to the boys at the gate,
And he pitched a great fast ball right over the plate.
Then Avi threw curve balls – some high and some low,
He kept those balls flying – some fast and some slow.

"You're good!" Yossi said, "You really can throw.
Will you join our ballgame? You pitch like a pro!
Come in for a snack, and after we eat,
There's a game in the park at the end of our street."

"You bet I'll be there," Avi said with a grin.
"I can't wait to play, and I hope that we win!"

Laibel whispered to Yossi, "What will our friends say?
Why on earth did you have to invite him to play?
The other team's coming from way across town.
How can we use a pitcher who plays sitting down?"

Just then came a squeal of delight by their side –
Avi was giving their baby a ride!
The boys looked at Esti, still tiny and new,
They watched Avi making her gurgle and coo.
He smiled at her, and she smiled right back.
"You see," Yossi said, "Esti's on the right track.

"Just look at our baby – she doesn't care
If our friend's on his feet or he sits in a chair.
If one kid has freckles, one's short and one's tall,
If one's missing a tooth, she won't notice at all!
If one kid has braces that shine in his smile
If one kid runs quickly and one takes a while,

If one friend wears glasses in order to see
Or another keeps trying, but can't sing on key,
A baby will make friends with anyone nice
She'll play with them all, and she'll never think twice.
You can learn from a baby what counts in the end,
It's what someone's like inside that makes him a friend!"

"Learn from a baby," laughed Laibel, "that's true!
I guess she can teach us a smart thing or two."
"Come on, Avi," he yelled as he jumped to his feet,
"We've got places to go; we've got people to meet.

"Our friends will be waiting; no two are the same
You'll see for yourself when we get to the game.
But how someone looks doesn't count in the end,
It's what he's like inside that makes him a friend!"

At the park down the street, boys were sitting around
No one was smiling or making a sound.
Their shoulders were sagging; their faces were glum.
"Guess what?" they grumbled. "Our pitcher can't come!
He's home, sick in bed, with a fever and flu
Should we cancel our ballgame? What else can we do?"

"Don't worry," said Laibel, a smile on his face,
"I know the right person to pitch in his place!
This is Avi, my neighbor. He moved in today,
Just wait till you guys see how well he can play!"

They stood for a minute; they stood there for two,
Thinking and wondering what they should do.
Avi just didn't look like a ball-playing guy
Should they let him join in? Should they give it a try?

The boys smiled at Avi; he grinned at them all
And together they shouted, "Come on, let's play ball!"

The game that they played turned out greater than great,
Yossi and Laibel's team won – nine to eight!

They walked Avi home, cheering him all the way –
What a friend, what a guy, what a game, what a day!

Yossi and Laibel smiled, brother to brother,
Proud of their friends and so proud of each other.
Laibel said, "Yossi, I see in the end,
It's what someone's like inside that makes him a friend!"